Vietnamese Children's
FAVORITE STORIES

Vietnamese Children's
FAVORITE STORIES

Retold by Tran Thi Minh Phuoc
Illustrated by Nguyen Thi Hop & Nguyen Dong

TUTTLE Publishing

Tokyo | Rutland, Vermont | Singapore

The Tuttle Story: "Books to Span the East and West"

Many people are surprised to learn that the world's largest publisher of books on Asia had its humble beginnings in the tiny American state of Vermont. The company's founder, Charles E. Tuttle, belonged to a New England family steeped in publishing.

Tuttle's father was a noted antiquarian dealer in Rutland, Vermont. Young Charles honed his knowledge of the trade working in the family bookstore, and later in the rare books section of Columbia University Library. His passion for beautiful books—old and new—never wavered throughout his long career as a bookseller and publisher.

After graduating from Harvard, Tuttle enlisted in the military and in 1945 was sent to Tokyo to work on General Douglas MacArthur's staff. He was tasked with helping to revive the Japanese publishing industry, which had been utterly devastated by the war. After his tour of duty was completed, he left the military, married a talented and beautiful singer, Reiko Chiba, and in 1948 began several successful business ventures.

To his astonishment, Tuttle discovered that postwar Tokyo was actually a book-lover's paradise. He befriended dealers in the Kanda district and began supplying rare Japanese editions to American libraries. He also imported American books to sell to the thousands of GIs stationed in Japan. By 1949, Tuttle's business was thriving, and he opened Tokyo's very first English-language bookstore in the Takashimaya Department Store in Ginza, to great success. Two years later, he began publishing books to fulfill the growing interest of foreigners in all things Asian.

Though a westerner, Tuttle was hugely instrumental in bringing a knowledge of Japan and Asia to a world hungry for information about the East. By the time of his death in 1993, he had published over 6,000 books on Asian culture, history and art—a legacy honored by Emperor Hirohito in 1983 with the "Order of the Sacred Treasure," the highest honor Japan can bestow upon a non-Japanese.

The Tuttle company today maintains an active backlist of some 1,500 titles, many of which have been continuously in print since the 1950s and 1960s—a great testament to Charles Tuttle's skill as a publisher. More than 60 years after its founding, Tuttle Publishing is more active today than at any time in its history, still inspired by Charles Tuttle's core mission—to publish fine books to span the East and West and provide a greater understanding of each.

Published by Tuttle Publishing,
an imprint of Periplus Editions (HK) Ltd.

www.tuttlepublishing.com

Library of Congress Cataloging-in-Publication Data
for this title is in progress
ISBN 978-0-8048-4429-1

19 18 17 16 15   5 4 3 2 1   1410TW
Printed in Malaysia

Distributed by

North America, Latin America & Europe
Tuttle Publishing
364 Innovation Drive,
North Clarendon,
VT 05759-9436 U.S.A.
Tel: (802) 773-8930
Fax: (802) 773-6993
info@tuttlepublishing.com
www.tuttlepublishing.com

Asia Pacific
Berkeley Books Pte. Ltd.
61 Tai Seng Avenue #02-12
Singapore 534167
Tel: (65) 6280-1330
Fax: (65) 6280-6290
inquiries@periplus.com.sg
www.periplus.com

Contents

Introduction

In Vietnam no Lunar New Year celebration (or *Tet Nguyen Dan*) can begin without a yellow Mai flower tree in the garden, or full blossoming branches of bright yellow Mai flowers in the house. The Mai flower represents good luck, happiness, and prosperity, and wards off evil spirits for the whole year. During the last days of Tet, every house is given a thorough cleaning, but it is important not to sweep away trash and the remains of burned firecrackers on the three New Year days, because to do so would also be to sweep away good luck and the hope of financial prosperity in the coming year. The broom itself is treated as a member of the family—never tossed aside or placed on the ground.

Why are such traditions so strong and enduring? I believe it is because the stories that explain traditions and beliefs have tremendous power to stir the imagination and touch the heart in ways that last forever. Our stories about our gods, heroes (both the mighty and the simple) and practices are a deep-seated part of who and what we are.

As a librarian and storyteller, I have been privileged to bring to life, for listeners of all ages, fascinating tales and legends from around the world. The Vietnamese legends and folktales presented in this book are some that are most dear to my heart. Some reflect our humorous way of explaining the ways of nature while others extol the virtues of the heroes of our legends. All of them paint a picture of a world that values the five great virtues: *Nhan* (Compassion), *Le* (Rituals), *Nghia* (Righteousness), *Tri* (Wisdom), and *Tin* (Trust).

It was through oral stories that my parents taught my siblings and me how to value virtue and live honorable lives. It was through traditional folktales that our grandparents taught us the morals we strive to apply and pass down to the younger generation.

Today, with so many Vietnamese-born forced to live so far from their native home, I use Vietnamese legends and folktales to help Vietnamese children learn about the land of their ancestors, its people, culture, and values. These stories connect them to a part of themselves that is indelible regardless of where they were born and how many generations removed they are from the land of their forebears. The fact that children of many backgrounds listen to and love these stories says much about the basic kinship we all share.

America is a land made of many immigrant families. While the first generation has a strong connection to their heritage, the language and culture gap between generations can all too easily widen over time. It is my hope that these stories—and the stories of all peoples—will foster bonds between generations and become a vehicle for bridging gaps between cultures as well.

—*Tran Thi Minh Phuoc*

The Legend of Banh Chung and Banh Day

In his old age, King Hung Vuong the Sixth, a mighty and brave warrior, decided one day to choose a successor. He thought to himself, "It won't be easy to choose amongst my twenty-two sons. I must be very careful in choosing the one who will rule after me."

The king was right. Just like their father, the princes were strong warriors, wise ambassadors, and ambitious adventurers. However, Prince Tiet Lieu, the eighteenth son, was not interested in hunting or in practicing martial arts like his brothers. Instead, he spent his time reading books and taking walks in the imperial court. The bonsai garden was the prince's favorite spot, and he could spend hours and hours pruning the miniature plants. One day, he asked the king to allow him to move with his wife and children to his mother's old village, where he could live the simple, humble life that suited him.

Toward the end of the year everyone began preparing traditional dishes to celebrate Tet. The royal court planned several ritual ceremonies to pay homage to the ancestors. Suddenly the king had an idea for discovering who would be worthiest of the throne. He summoned all the princes and announced, "In three days, whoever brings the best dish to offer our ancestors for the New Year will be my successor."

The princes set out in the quest for rare and exotic foods. The oldest prince climbed up to the top of the mountain and navigated through dark caves to harvest the swallows' nests. Some of the other princes went deep into the jungle for rare mushrooms and herbs, or deep down into the sea to seek out abalone and choice seafood from amongst the reef beds. Others sought advice for the best recipes.

On his way home, Prince Tiet Lieu felt sad because he couldn't travel far like his brothers. As he walked along the rice fields, the fresh and relaxing aroma of the rice and the heartfelt laughter of the farmers lessened his grief. Suddenly a thought came to him. "Rice! This precious grain feeds us all, from the richest of us to the poorest. My dish should be prepared from this!" And the prince rushed back home, full of excitement.

That night, as he slept, the prince dreamt of a fairy who showed him how to prepare the wonderful dish to offer to the ancestors. "You don't need to go far—use your own hands, mind and heart, and food harvested from your own lands to make rice cakes. You will rule the kingdom peacefully and gloriously," the fairy said.

"Thank you!" the prince cried. "I will never forget your great advice and kindness."

At dawn, the prince was awakened by the rooster's crowing. Quickly he woke his wife and shared his dream. Together they went outside, looked up at the open sky, and thanked the fairy for her blessings. "We don't have much time!" said the prince. "Let's make square and round rice cakes to offer to our ancestors."

While his wife ground the sweet rice and prepared the meat, the prince went to the field and cut dong leaves to use as cake wrappers. Their children washed and soaked the mung beans. After long hours of cooking, the whole family was happy to have beautiful cakes. They called them Banh Chung and Banh Day.

On New Year's Eve, all the princes rushed back to the kingdom with exquisite and rare dishes. The king eagerly tasted every single dish and learned its meaning. Nothing tasted good to him. Then he noticed the square green and round white cakes from Prince Tiet Lieu, which he had never before seen or tasted, at the far end of the table.

"How did you come up with this dish?" asked the king.

The prince told the King about his dream and explained, "The green dong leaves and bamboo strings wrapping the cakes represent the protection and safety of family and home. The yellow mung beans and marinated meat stuffing represent the animals and plants on the Earth and the food they provide for all. The square Banh Chung is our mother the Earth, and the round white Banh Day is the Heaven Sky."

The king tasted both cakes and found them delicious, savory, and meaningful. And so, greatly contented, he joyfully proclaimed Prince Tiet Lieu successor to the throne, and he declared that, from that day on, the Banh Chung and Banh Day would be the traditional food offered to the ancestors during Tet.

Mai An Tiem and the Watermelon Seeds

Long ago, during the Hung Dynasty, there was a wise and hard-working orphan named Mai An Tiem who earned a meager living helping an elderly couple who lived nearby.

One summer day, King Hung and his royal court rode through Phong Chau and were told great tales about the orphan. Moved by the orphan's warm heart, the king decided to adopt the young boy and bring him to his kingdom.

As the years passed, Mai An Tiem grew up to be a strong and brave man. He proved himself worthy to the king, who admired his virtues and values. The king gave him great love, support, and protection. He even gave his daughter's hand to Mai An Tiem and gave the couple many rare and precious gifts.

One day, Mai An Tiem invited the princes to his house for a feast. Everyone enjoyed the company and took turns sharing stories. The eldest prince said how powerful and lucky he was because he was born first and expected to be the king's successor. The second prince jumped in by stating that the king needed a strong successor to protect the kingdom. Stories went on and on and on....

Everyone knew that the king loved and admired Mai An Tiem the most, and they were eager to hear his story. "As always, I believe in learning how to be happy and successful with what I have. I am grateful for the blessings of wealth, love, and power from the king, but it doesn't change who I am," said Mai An Tiem humbly.

The youngest prince, always jealous when he saw his father's special favors to his adopted son, rushed back to the kingdom and told a different story, saying that Mai An Tiem was arrogant, unfaithful, ambitious, and disrespectful to the king, and hoped to overthrow him.

Infuriated, the king ordered his soldiers to take Mai An Tiem and his family to a deserted island with nothing but his old blade and some dry seeds. The king wanted to punish the arrogant and unfaithful adopted son. "Let's see if he can live without my help and blessings!" he cried.

The next day, Mai An Tiem and his family left the kingdom escorted by the royal soldiers. After three days they reached the island. "Please convey my deepest gratitude and respect to the king for his constant blessings, generosity, and kindness to me and my family," Mai An Tiem said to one of the soldiers. The royal soldiers returned to the kingdom.

It was dark and chilly that night. Mai An Tiem could find no shelter but a cave by the shore. "Let's stay here for tonight; it will protect us from the cold winds and wild animals," Mai An Tiem said to his wife.

The next morning, Mai An Tiem woke up early. He went along the shore to collect seaweed, then up to the hill for firewood. Deep in the forest, with his old blade he cut bamboo stalks for building a house and bamboo shoots for food.

Four years passed. The children grew up fast. They learned to find beans and other vegetables and grow them in a garden. Mai An Tiem spent a lot of time tilling the rocky soil and went fishing. His wife made some warm clothes from animal skins and prepared hearty dishes. Their life was stable.

One day, while resting on the hill, Mai An Tiem saw a flock of crows flying by the island, croaking and cawing angrily. Suddenly he noticed something falling down from the sky. He ran up to the hill and, surprisingly, spotted some black seeds scattered everywhere. He collected them all and chose a good spot on the hill to plant them.

Before long, the whole hill was covered with strong green vines, bright yellow flowers, and many big, strange round fruits of all sizes.

"I don't know if this fruit is edible, or how to eat it," said the wife.

"Crows dropped the seeds from the sky, and if birds can eat it, we can eat it as well," Mai An Tiem replied.

Then he chose the biggest fruit and cut it in half. To his surprise, inside the green rind was bright red pulp dotted with black seeds.

The fruit was so juicy and sweet. "Let's name it Dua Hau because it tastes like melon," said Mai An Tiem.

Excited by the new fruit, they used the seeds to plant another crop. Within months, they harvested more big melons. One day, while collecting seaweed, Mai An Tiem had an idea. He ran back to the melon hill, selected a half dozen of the melons, and carved his name and a map of the island on the green rind. He rushed back to the shore and set the melons adrift in the sea in the hope that a sailor would find it.

Every week, more melons were thrown in the sea until, one day, a merchant ship came to the island and looked for the owner of these delicious fruits.

Many more ships came to buy the exotic fruits. Mai An Tiem's life became busier and more comfortable. With the merchant's help, he was able to send the finest melons to the king.

One day, among the exotic dishes, the king noticed fresh slices of red fruit dotted with black seeds. He had never before seen such a fruit. He tried one piece and enjoyed it very much. When he asked about the source of the fruit, and learned of the island from which it came and of the man who sent it, the king realized that the giver of the wonderful fruit was his exiled adopted son.

Touched by Mai An Tiem's loyalty and generosity, the king ordered the soldiers to bring his family back to the kingdom. He regretted that he had misjudged his adopted son. "Mai An Tiem is right—through good times or tough times, nothing changes who he is. He deserves to be blessed!" the king proclaimed. Since that day Dua Hau, or watermelons, were planted throughout the kingdom to honor Mai An Tiem.

The Legend of the Mai Flower

There would be no Tet (or, Tet Nguyen Dan) without a yellow Mai flower tree in the front yard, or blossoming branches of bright Mai flowers in the house to bring good luck, happiness, and prosperity.

According to the legend, the Mai flower was once a brave little girl who lived happily with her parents and sister in a small village. They loved each other dearly. Everyone knew that the little girl's favorite color was yellow and that she loved nature. Unlike her big sister, who was always by her mother's side, the little girl spent most of her days with her father in the forest, hunting and cutting wood. In the evening she loved to talk and share stories with the Kitchen Gods, to whom she was grateful for the delicious and nourishing meals they gave.

One day, the oldest Kitchen God talked about his annual trip to the heavens. He thought it would be perfect if the Kitchen Gods could ride on a yellow carp. "Don't worry, Mr. Kitchen God. We can get one for you. My sister is great at catching fishes in the pond," said the little girl happily. True to her word, a yellow carp was on the Kitchen Gods' altar that very evening.

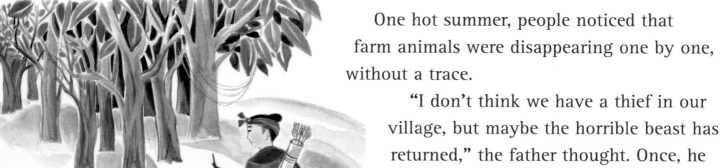

One hot summer, people noticed that farm animals were disappearing one by one, without a trace.

"I don't think we have a thief in our village, but maybe the horrible beast has returned," the father thought. Once, he had chased a severely wounded beast into a cave, and the villagers covered the opening with heavy boulders. "But he should be dead by now," the father thought.

From then on, farmers left the rice fields early and rushed the animals back to the barn before dusk for fear they'd be attacked and eaten by the beast. Everyone was afraid to cross the forest at night except for the girl's father. He was a good hunter, a brave monster fighter, and a great runner. He was the most admired protector of the village, having conquered other beasts and monsters in the past.

The hunter and his daughter, accompanied by strong farmers, went out early one morning in search of the beast.

"It's time to bring peace to our village,"

the hunter said. He ordered everyone, including his little girl, to stay behind and wait for him by the mountain.

"Father, please let me stay near you. I want to be there if you need help," the little girl begged. The father, pleased by her bravery, agreed to let her join in the battle.

The little girl went through the forest, carefully following her father's instructions, and found the beast's cave almost instantly. The monster appeared to be half-human, half-snake. He moved so fast that all the trees and branches were broken and destroyed. He roared with rage at the sight the hunter and his little girl.

The battle began and went on for hours. Finally, with a great shriek, the beast fell to the ground. Its tail knocked the girl very hard into the cave. Everyone was relieved that the beast was dead, but grieved because there was no sign of the little girl. She was buried among the rocks where no one could see her but the oldest Kitchen God.

The girl begged the oldest Kitchen God, who was returning to the heavens, to ask the Heaven God to restore her life so that she could be with her family again. Moved by her bravery and steadfastness, the Heaven God granted her wish, but he could not let her stay on earth forever. She could return to earth only for nine days every year, during Tet.

After her parents and sister passed away, the little girl came back to earth for the very last time, left her yellow blouse by the front gate, and disappeared. The following year, villagers found a magnificent tree bearing bright yellow flowers at the front gate. Surprisingly, the fragrant flowers appeared only for nine days, then were replaced by green buds and leaves. They named it the Mai to remember the brave and lovely little girl.

Why One Shouldn't Sweep the House On Tet Nguyen Dan

Vietnamese people have many little myths and superstitions. For example, they believe that good fortune will come to a neat house. All brooms, dusting brushes, and dustpans are hidden away after the last cleaning before New Year's Eve, which is also known as Giao Thua. One should promptly pick up any broom laid on the ground and lean its handle against the wall for good luck. People don't sweep the house during the first three days of Tet for fear of getting rid of luck and fortune. Rubbish, especially the debris of red firecrackers, is kept in pile in a corner of the house before it is carried out through the back door on the fifth day of the New Year. Why are sweeping and cleaning prohibited on the New Year's days?

According to legend, there was a trader named Au Minh who lived in a boathouse near a fishing village. Trading began early in the morning in the floating market. Every day Au Minh sailed along the river and cruised between the farmers' small boats to buy their goods, which were hung on the pole in front of each boat to attract customers from a distance.

Au Minh was a good trader and bargainer. He managed quite well, on very little money, to buy merchandise and resell it quickly. Unfortunately, he couldn't compete with the richer traders, and so by sunrise he would head back to shore, helping the fishermen to clean fish or repair their nets.

Often the poor trader helped the villagers set up altars for ritual ceremonies. He would pray to Thuy Than, the Goddess of Waters, to protect fishermen in high seas from bad weather and to bless them with a bountiful catch. During drought, he would ask Ong Sam, the Thunder God, and Ba Set, the Lightning Goddess, for more rain so the farmers could grow their crops.

One hot summer day, as he was passing by the lake, Au Minh met the Goddess of Waters, who gave him a little girl named Nhu Nguyen, which means "As You Wish." He shouted with glee, "Thank you for your blessing! I promise to raise her as my own daughter."

Au Minh was very fortunate to have Nhu Nguyen around. The father and daughter worked hard and traded more goods. As the years passed, Nhu Nguyen grew up to be a beautiful, kind, and sensible young lady. She was a big help in the house and a good cook as well. Au Minh became richer and richer. He bought a big house and employed people to work for him.

It was New Year's Eve. Au Minh decorated his house with spring couplets and red banners. He hung two long strings of fireworks in front of the house to welcome the New Year and ward off bad spirits. Two big kumquat plants, symbols of a happy family, brightened the entire house. The ancestors' altar was filled with candied fruits, a five-fruits tray, rice cakes, and joss sticks. Nhu Nguyen was busy arranging the yellow Mai flowers, colorful chrysanthemums, fresh marigolds, and fragrant narcissi.

As he swept and cleaned the front yard, Au Minh heard a loud crash. He ran quickly to the house and saw Nhu Nguyen picking up the flowers splattered all over the wet floor amongst pieces of broken porcelain.

Out of anger and frustration, he threw the broom at Nhu Nguyen and shouted at the top of his lungs, "Out of my house! You're so careless, you broke my most valuable vase!"

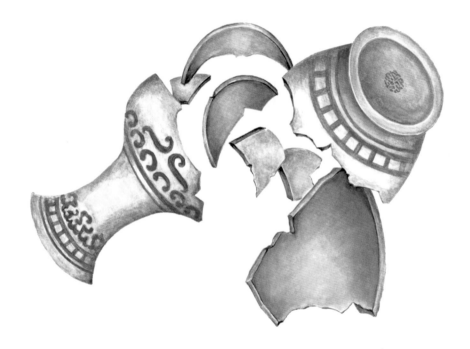

Terrified and heartbroken, Nhu Nguyen ran out the back door and hid in the rubbish heap. Au Minh chased after her and searched through the rubbish heap with the big broom. But he found nothing, and with all his might, he swept the heap into the river. Tet was coming, but Au Minh couldn't find his daughter anywhere in the house.

Since that day, the miserable Au Minh had no luck in his business. All his employees and servants left him. Finally, he sold his house and became as poor as he was before. He didn't realize that that he had swept Than Tai, the God of Fortune, out of his house when he chased Nhu Nguyen away.

Today, one can find the altar of Than Tai placed on the floor in the corner of the house or by the entrance of a restaurant or business office for good luck and fortune.

Le Loi and the Magic Sword

In Vietnam there is a lake that glows with a special light, and in its middle is a temple dedicated to a great hero.

   Centuries ago, during the period in China known as the Ming Dynasty, China invaded Vietnam and, for a time, Vietnam was subjected to Chinese rule. Vietnamese culture was pushed aside as the people were forced to take on Chinese ways. In the mines and fields people were forced to work to enrich China's treasury. Their anger and unhappiness grew until, at last, they gathered together to try to overthrow their oppressive rulers.

One of the leaders of the revolt was the brave Le Loi, an honorable nobleman in the village of Lam Son in the Thanh Hoa province. Even the Chinese respected him, and invited him to become an official, or mandarin. But, loyal to his own people, Le Loi refused. Instead, he recruited and trained fighters against the Chinese. Although they were defeated time and time again, Le Loi and his fighters never gave up.

As the fighting raged on, a fisherman named Le Than carried on his humble work, rowing out day after day, casting his nets wide in hopes of a good catch.

One day Le Than felt something unusually heavy in his fishing net. Excited at the thought of catching a large fish, he eagerly pulled in the net, but was disappointed to see a long, thin metal blade. He threw the blade back into the water. However, each time he cast his net, the tug that he thought would be a host of fish was again and again the mysterious blade.

"What is happening? Why does this blade always return to my net?" the fisherman sighed in despair. At last Le Than decided that, since the blade refused to be cast away, he would have to keep it. He took it home and kept it in a corner of his hut.

Years later, Le Than joined Le Loi's army to fight against the Chinese. Le Than proved to be a cunning warrior, and Le Loi often visited his home to discuss strategy.

During one visit, Le Loi noticed something glowing in the corner of Le Than's hut. Le Loi approached the glowing light and saw that it came from the blade Le Than had pulled from the water years ago. As Le Loi held up the blade to inspect it, two words magically appeared on the blade: "Thuan Thien," which meant "Will of Heaven." Le Loi believed this was a gift from the heavens, and Le Than was honored to gave the blade to him.

Le Loi continued to lead his men into battle, but his troops were small, many of his men were inexperienced, and food was scarce—and all of these things led to constant defeat. Many of the fighters left the army, and the resistance movement became weaker and weaker. Le Loi, a few officers, and their handful of remaining soldiers finally withdrew into the Chi Linh mountains.

One day, while trying to hide from approaching enemy troops, Le Loi climbed a tall banyan tree. While in the tree, he saw a strange light gleaming from its branches. As he crept nearer he saw, tangled in the banyan tree's branches, the bladeless hilt of a sword. The hilt was encrusted with many precious jewels.

At once Le Loi knew this was the hilt destined for the blade given to him from the heavens through Le Than. When he put the blade and hilt together, they fit perfectly!

As Le Loi held his sacred sword high in the air he felt as strong as a thousand men. He could hear the sound of the galloping horses and the rattling of invaders' chariots. He could feel the agony and sufferings of his people throughout the country under the harsh rule of the Chinese. He knew that the heavens had entrusted him with the task of using the sword to defeat the invaders and free his people. He knelt on the ground, looked up into the sky, and said solemnly, "Thank you, Lord, for giving me strength, courage, power and patience to conquer our enemies and drive them from our land."

Le Loi recruited more soldiers than ever to his army in the mountains and led them to victory, winning each battle efforlessly with the help of his magic sword. Before long, the Vietnamese people were free from Chinese rule. There was no sign of the enemy in the country, and the men returned home and lived happily and peacefully with their families.

Because of his wisdom and his courage Le Loi became the Emperor Le Thai To. Vietnam became a mighty land under his kind and gentle rule. He was highly respected and loved by everyone.

One beautiful day, Le Loi was rowing his Thuyen Rong (Dragon Boat) on Ho Luc Thuy, also called the Green Water Lake since the water was green all year round. As Le Loi felt the sun's rays on his face and listened to the soothing sounds of the water hitting his boat, Kim Quy, a giant turtle with a golden shell, emerged from the water. To Le Loi's surprise, Kim Quy began to speak.

"Le Loi, the heavens are pleased that you have restored freedom and peace to your people. But now it is time for you to return the magical sword to its owner, Long Vuong the Dragon King."

Le Loi thanked the turtle and its master for lending the sword and carefully placed it in the turtle's mouth, and the turtle dove quickly to the bottom of the lake. Thereafter, the lake was called Ho Hoan Kiem, or the Lake of the Returned Sword. To this day one can see the glowing light of the magical sword beneath the water.

Among his other titles, Le Loi became known as Binh Dinh Vuong, which means King of Pacification. He is the founder of the Le Dynasty, which ruled Vietnam for more than three hundred years, and is one of the greatest heroes the land has ever known.

The Celestial King Phu Dong and the Iron Horse

Long ago in the northern province of Bac Ninh, in a small village called Phu Dong, there lived a very kindly couple. They had been married for many years and worked hard in the rice fields, but had not been blessed with a child. While they were content with their humble life, they still longed for a son or daughter.

One day while working in the rice fields, the wife saw large footprints in the wet mud. "Oh my! Who could have such large feet!" she exclaimed. As she stepped inside the footprints to compare them to her own feet, she felt a tingling sensation throughout her body. Intrigued by this strange sensation, she went home to tell her husband.

A few weeks later, the wife noticed her belly getting bigger and bigger. She and her husband quickly realized she was pregnant, and they were overjoyed. The elderly couple thanked the Lord for granting their sole wish. In time they gave birth to a charming boy they named Giong.

They adored the boy and took good care of him, but Giong was a strange baby. He was very small and never seemed to grow. He never smiled or spoke.

Three years passed, Giong couldn't crawl, roll over, or walk. He would spend his days just eating and sleeping. But his parents still loved him dearly. "Someday, you will grow up to be a fine man!" whispered the mother to her baby.

For years the people of the Phu Dong village lived in peace. Then one day the invaders from the north launched an attack on the Van Lang kingdom. The king sent many soldiers to protect the northern border, but the invaders were too strong. The enemies destroyed many villages and kept on advancing. In desperation, the king sent his ambassadors to all of the villages in search of strong, brave men to join the fight.

One day, the ambassador reached the village of Phu Dong. His announcement quickly spread throughout the village, and the men of the village prepared for battle. When word reached the home of the young Giong, the boy astonished his parents by suddenly sitting up and speaking for the first time. "Mother and Father, please invite the ambassador to our home so I can speak with him."

When the ambassador reached Giong's home, he was amazed that a toddler could speak so eloquently. "Sir, I have a request," began Giong. "Please tell the king to make me an iron suit of armor, a metal conical hat, a long sword, and an iron horse that would fit a giant! Bring these things as quickly as you can and I will help you defeat the invaders!"

The ambassador knew that the Heavens must have sent this young child to be a protector of the kingdom. He gratefully replied, "Yes, I swear I will return with the things you need."

Without wasting another minute the ambassador returned to the king and reported what he saw and heard. Overjoyed, the king summoned all the blacksmiths. "Gather all of the iron in the kingdom and make me the finest suit of armor, the sharpest sword, the strongest hat, and the most magnificent iron horse! Make all of these fit for a giant!"

For three days and nights, all of the blacksmiths worked hard to finish these things for Giong.

Meanwhile, in Phu Dong, Giong was preparing for battle. He said, "Mother, Father, thank you for taking such good care of me these past three years. It is now my turn to take care of you and our people. Please bring me food so I can become strong, and new clothes for my growing body."

All of the villagers quickly rushed to gather rice, veggies, and fresh fish. Giong's mother gathered up all the fabric in the village and began sewing new clothes for Giong. Food was brought and Giong devoured it all. Bowl after bowl of rice disappeared almost instantly. The fish was gone as soon as it went from the pan to his plate.

With each bite Giong took, he grew. He stretched his shoulders and, before long, Giong was the size of a great tree. As he put on his new clothes, the king's men arrived with his new armor, a long sharp sword, a strong hat, and a beautiful iron horse.

"I am ready to do battle to protect our land!" exclaimed Giong as he mounted his horse. With one giant leap, Giong rode his horse over the village and into the forest where the enemy was waiting. Fiery flames shot out of his horse's nostrils as Giong chased his enemies back. The flames from his iron horse marred the bamboo fields. With each swipe of his mighty blade, the other army drew back in fear. Suddenly, Giong's sword was broken. Quickly the brave warrior uprooted the tall bamboo and used it to fight back the invaders. Before long, the northern invaders surrendered to the brave and mighty warrior.

Giong returned home and said farewell to his parents and the villagers. Then he rode straight to Soc Mountain, removed his armor and gave a bow to Mother Earth before leaping into the heavens with his iron horse. The king and people of Vietnam were very thankful for Giong's goodness and bravery. The king had a temple built at the Phu Dong village to honor Thanh Giong—or Saint Giong—and proclaimed him the warrior Phu Dong Thien Vuong—the Celestial King who was sent from the heavens to protect the people.

In Vietnam, every year on the ninth of April of the lunar calendar, people celebrate the festival of Saint Giong in memory of the heavens' messenger who fought against the invaders to save the country. It is said that lakes were formed around the giant horse's shoes where the warrior passed. Since that day, the bamboo called Tre Dang Nga grows yellow at the Phu Dong village because it was burnt by the iron horse's fiery breath.

Son Tinh and Thuy Tinh—the Mountain Lord and the Sea Lord

Long ago in Vietnam lived King Hung the Eighteenth of the Hong Bang dynasty. Not only was he regarded as a wise ruler, but he was also known for having a beautiful daughter, Princess My Nuong. Princess My Nuong was often considered fairylike with her shiny black hair, smooth fair skin, and graceful manner. She was a very charming and sweet tempered young princess. Many suitors from faraway lands came seeking My Nuong's hand in marriage but the king and the queen did not find any of them worthy enough. They wanted someone strong, brave, intelligent, and talented for My Nuong.

One day, two young extraordinary men came to the palace with marriage proposals for My Nuong. One was Son Tinh, the Mountain Lord, and the other was Thuy Tinh, the Sea Lord. King Hung was very impressed with both of them. Each was prestigious, powerful, and worthy of My Nuong.

"If you choose me, your daughter will help me rule the vast mountains!" exclaimed Son Tinh. "I control all of the forest animals, majestic trees, and prized jewels. With me, she would be guaranteed a peaceful and prosperous life!"

"If you choose me, your daughter will be the queen of the seas!" countered Thuy Tinh. "I rule the vast oceans and the creatures within it! I have beautiful gems, coral, and pearls. I can command the rains, the thunder, the storms, and strong winds to nourish and protect your kingdom. A life with me would be a life of happiness and comfort."

The king admired these talented men and wanted to see more of their powers. Immediately the Sea Lord raised his right arm to conduct the elements of wind and rain. The whole court could hear the loud roll and crack of thunder as torrential rains poured down. Then, in an instant, all was quiet and peaceful again as the Sea Lord raised his left arm and stopped the storm. "Wow, that was frightening!" one of the mandarins exclaimed. "How powerful Thuy Tinh is!"

Now, it was the Mountain Lord's turn. He took a deep breath and closed his eyes. Within seconds, the whole royal court could listen to soft breezes blowing, enjoy the sweet chirping of birds and singing of crickets, and smell the most fragrant fresh flowers. Then he opened his eyes and everything returned to normal. Everyone in the kingdom felt very calm and rested.

King Hung had a very hard time deciding between two such worthy and talented suitors. "Please go and gather your wedding gifts for My Nuong." he said. "Tomorrow, whoever returns first will be given her hand in marriage." The queen praised her husband for his wise decision.

Without wasting a second, Son Tinh and Thuy Tinh rushed off to get their gifts. Son Tinh called all of the forest creatures to help. The monkeys helped pick the ripest and most delicious lychees, dragon fruits, peaches, and Buddha's hand fruit. The elephants helped gather precious jewels and metals from the caves. The sparrows gathered the most fragrant and colorful flowers.

Meanwhile, Thuy Tinh summoned all of the sea creatures to aid him. The oysters gave him their largest and shiniest pearls. The sharks gathered the freshest fish, shrimp, and crab. The lobsters harvested the succulent seaweed.

All day and night, Son Tinh and Thuy Tinh worked diligently to gather all of their special gifts.

Just as the sun began to rise the next day, Son Tinh arrived at King Hung's palace with his gifts: baskets and baskets of ripe fruit, beautiful jewels and gems, vibrant flowers to fill the palace, nine beautiful wild horses, and a pair of rare blue phoenix. King Hung and the queen were deeply impressed by the magnificent and rare gifts.

True to his word, the king gave My Nuong's hand in marriage to Son Tinh. My Nuong said goodbye to her parents and happily went to the Tan Vien mountain to live with her new husband.

Shortly after the new couple left, Thuy Tinh arrived with his gifts. "I am so sorry, Thuy Tinh," King Hung said. "Son Tinh arrived before you and, as I promised, My Nuong is now his wife."

Devastated, Thuy Tinh dropped to his knees and shouted angrily, "No! I should have been the one to marry the princess! And I will have her, no matter what it takes! Beware my wrath, Son Tinh!"

Full of rage, he jumped to his feet and sprang from the palace. He hated losing, and he truly wanted My Nuong as his wife. He summoned all of his warriors to attack Son Tinh, who was on his way home with Princess My Nuong.

Son Tinh sent down his own fierce army to fight off Thuy Tinh, who had called up the sea to flood all the mountains and forests.

For many days and nights, the two armies fought furiously. Thuy Tinh would send strong waves and thundering storms to attack Son Tinh, who would keep retreating higher and higher into the mountains. Plants and trees were blown away. Land was trampled and destroyed. Son Tinh used his power to raise the mountains higher, so that people and homes were not washed away. After countless days of fighting, with no sign of victory in sight for either side, Thuy Tinh decided to stop fighting, withdrew his water, and returned to the sea.

But Thuy Tinh was not ready to completely give up the fight. Each year he would try to attack Son Tinh, sending humongous waves, deafening thunder, strong typhoons, and heavy rainstorms in order to get My Nuong. This rainy period lasting from July to August has been known as the monsoon season in Vietnam, and occurs each year as Son Tinh and Thuy Tinh fight for My Nuong.

The Story of Tam and Cam

Long ago in a small village there lived a sweet, kind young girl named Tam.
After her mother died, she and her father lived alone together, but one day,
Tam's father married again. His new wife was a widow who also had a young
daughter, named Cam. For a few years, the four of them lived together peacefully.
But when her father passed away, everything changed for Tam.

Tam's stepmother was mean and selfish. She
doted on Cam but ignored and
abused poor Tam. All day
long, Tam watered the
manioc roots and harvested
golden yams while Cam
chased butterflies and
picked wild flowers.

Tam worked hard and never complained. Over time, she grew into a beautiful young woman. Her stepmother, jealous for her own daughter, wanted to hide Tam's beauty. She gave her tattered clothes to wear and sent her to work long hours in the sun so that her skin would become dry and ruddy, and gave her only leftover scraps and unripe bananas to eat.

One day the stepmother sent the girls to the river to catch fish. "Come home with your basket full or you will have no supper," she threatened. The girls went to the river and, as usual, Tam worked hard while Cam basked in the sun. Several hours later, Tam's basket was full of fish and Cam's was empty.

Cam was just as mean-spirited as her mother and said to Tam, "Sister, your hair is so dirty. You should go wash it before we go home, or else mother will be angry." When Tam went to the water to wash her hair, Cam quickly dumped all of Tam's fish into her own basket and hurried home. When Tam returned and saw her empty basket, she wept because she knew she would be punished.

Suddenly a beautiful fairy appeared before her. "Don't cry, child, but look in your basket. See this little fish? Look after it, and only good things will come to you." Tam looked into her basket and saw a little orange fish. She named him "Bong" and kept him in a little pond in the yard, secretly bringing him a few grains of rice each day. For weeks, Tam would call out "Bong, come and eat!" and little Bong would come up and eagerly eat his rice. Tam was happy to have a new friend.

One day Cam and her mother saw Tam happily feeding Bong. Since they never wanted to see Tam happy, they hatched a wicked plan. "Come on, Mother, help me catch the fish. I want to eat it!" cried Cam. "Yes, my dear, we'll do it the moment Tam goes to work the field," replied the stepmother. As soon as Tam was away, Cam put on Tam's ragged clothes and rubbed dirt on her face, and called to the fish, "Bong, come and eat!" When Bong came to the surface, the stepmother and Cam caught him and cooked him.

When Tam came home she called out to her friend, "Bong, come and eat!" But Bong did not come. Tam looked around and saw fish bones near the pond, and sadly realized what had happened. She carefully buried the bones and said farewell to Bong.

Few days later Tam found a beautiful pair of red velvet embroidered shoes where Bong's bones had been buried. She knew they must have been a gift from Bong and the fairy. Tam was overjoyed! Never before had she owned anything so beautiful. She carefully tucked the shoes in her skirt pocket. Whenever she was alone in the field, safe from the eyes of others, she would put them on and imagine a happier life.

One morning, rain poured from the sky, and Tam ran as fast as she could to bring the cows and buffalos to the barn. While running, she dropped her beautiful shoes into the muddy pond. She carefully washed them in the river and hung them on the buffalo's horns to dry. Suddenly, one shoe was snatched by a raven, who carried it away and dropped in front of the king's palace.

Tam was devastated at the loss of her shoe, and took great care to keep her remaining shoe safe.

At the palace, the king stumbled upon Tam's shoe. He marveled at how delicate and beautiful it was. "Whoever can wear such a shoe must be as lovely and graceful as the shoe itself, and I must make her my wife!" he exclaimed. Thus, he sent out a proclamation that the maiden whose foot fit the shoe would become his queen.

Word quickly spread throughout the kingdom. When Tam heard the news, she thought, "This must be my missing shoe!" and begged her stepmother to allow her to try it on.

"You, ugly thing? You may not even leave this house until you finish sorting these grains!" the cruel stepmother shrieked. She mixed all the grain together in a huge basket and rushed off with Cam to meet the king's messenger.

As the heartbroken Tam began to weep the fairy appeared. "Don't worry, dear child. Help will come!" she cried. She summoned the ravens, who flew to Tam's side and, within minutes, had sorted every single grain. With cries of deepest gratitude, Tam happily rushed off to try on the shoe.

Many women were pushing and pulling, but no one's foot was tiny enough to fit the shoe. When Cam's turn came she squeezed with all of her might, but she could not force her foot into the shoe.

At last it was Tam's turn and, of course, the shoe fit her perfectly! Then she surprised everyone by pulling out the other red velvet shoe.

The messenger whisked Tam off to the king and they were married that day. From then on, Tam lived a happy life as queen, but never forgot the kind fairy or her dear friend Bong.

The Story of Thach Sanh and Ly Thong

Long ago, there lived a young boy named Thach Sanh. He worked hard alongside his parents, harvesting rice in the fields and chopping wood in the forest. Despite all of their hard work, the family remained very poor. Then, when Thach Sanh was in his teens, his parents passed away.

After selling his home and household goods to pay for his parents' funeral, Thach Sanh's only possession was his father's mighty axe with a blade that never dulled. He spent his days gathering wood and his nights sleeping under a large banyan tree.

One evening, a merchant named Ly Thong was traveling through the forest and saw Thach Sanh returning to the banyan tree.

"Hello young man! Do you live in the forest?" asked Ly Thong as he surveyed the young man dressed in tattered clothes.

"Yes, my name is Thach Sanh. I have been living in the forest and selling wood in the market since my parents passed away," was the reply. "My name is Ly Thong and I am a merchant," Ly Thong said. "I live with my elderly mother and we need extra help. You can live with us in exchange for food and shelter. We can be like brothers!"

Thach Sanh happily and gratefully agreed.

For months Thach Sanh worked hard helping Ly Thong and his elderly mother. Everything seemed perfect until a monster began to attack the village's local temple. The giant beast would come each night to break down walls and smash the statues.

The king was deeply vexed by all the destruction and declared that whoever could slay the beast would have a great reward. Until the beast could be destroyed, the villagers took turns guarding the temple each night.

Eventually Ly Thong's turn came, but he was a cowardly man and he asked Thach Sanh to go in his place. Thach Sanh had heard nothing about the monster, as he spent his days away at work in the forest. Ly Thong did not want to frighten him away from the task, so he didn't speak of the monster. Instead, he told Ly Thong that the temple needed to be protected against thieves.

That evening Thach Sanh headed to the temple with his mighty axe. As he sat outside the temple door he saw a great monster come out of the shadow. The monster was tremendously tall and had two large horns on its head.

Without hesitating, Thach Sanh swung his mighty axe. The defeated monster toppled to the ground. Thach Sanh quickly ran home to tell Ly Thong what happened. Ly Thong was a man who always dreamt of fame and fortune, and when he heard what had happened, he wanted to take credit.

"Thach Sanh my brother! That is the king's beast who guards the temple! When he hears you have killed it, he will punish you! Let me go talk to the king and ask for forgiveness. In the meantime, hide yourself. I will let you know when all is well," Ly Thong promised.

"Thank you brother!" Thach Sanh replied, not knowing he had been tricked. Thach Sanh went back to the banyan tree to hide while Ly Thong went to the king claiming he had defeated the beast. The king was grateful, and rewarded Ly Thong with many riches and with soldiers to command.

For weeks, Thach Sanh waited patiently in the woods. One morning, he saw a giant eagle flying overhead with a young woman screaming for help in its claws. Thach Sanh started to follow the eagle's path. What Thach Sanh did not know was the young woman was the princess, who had been kidnapped by the eagle. The king had sent all of the men of the village into the forest to rescue her. Whoever was successful would receive her hand in marriage.

Ly Thong was the fastest of the men, and as he was running he ran into Thach Sanh. "Brother! It is so good to see you! Is the king still angry? Did you see the eagle flying overhead with the woman? I was going to follow it and try to save her!" Thach Sanh said.

Ly Thong was already scheming and said, "Yes, brother! I will tell you all about it later! But let's not waste time now! Let's hurry to rescue the princess!"

54

The two men followed the eagle into a dark cave. As they ventured deep into the cave they spotted the princess. The eagle was guarding her. Thach Sanh quickly attacked the bird.

As Thach Sanh was bravely fighting the eagle, Ly Thong grabbed the princess and made his way to the exit. The princess was so frightened that she lost her ability to speak. As they left the cave, the devious Ly Thong called his soldiers to roll a boulder over entrance, saying that it was to trap the eagle, but it really was to trap Thach Sanh.

After a long fight Thach Sanh defeated the eagle. But it wasn't long before he realized that the entrance was blocked and he had no way out. For hours Thach Sanh navigated the dark caves. Following the sound of a voice moaning in the dark, he found a young man tied up in a corner of the cave.

"Please help me!" the man begged, "I am the Prince of the Sea and the evil eagle kidnapped me!"

Thach Sanh freed the prince and, with his help, pushed and pushed at the boulder that kept them captive in the cave. At last, after much pushing, they were free!

"Thank you for your kindness. Please accept this token of my gratitude," the prince said as he handed Thach Sanh a small wooden flute.

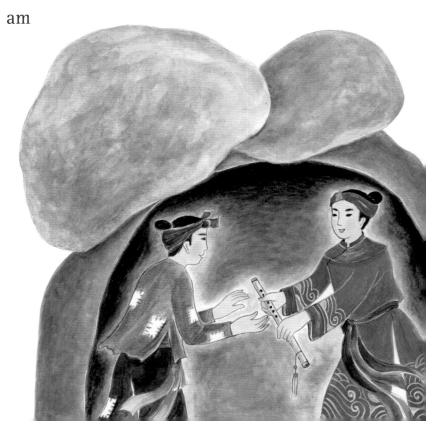

Thach Sanh thanked his new friend and made his way back to the palace. Meanwhile, at the palace, the king was overjoyed that his daughter has been rescued, but he was puzzled by her inability to speak.

"Ly Thong, you saved my daughter! As I promised, she will be your wife. But first you must find a doctor to help her regain her voice. Then I can give you your wedding," the king said.

As Ly Thong left the palace he saw Thach Sanh approaching and was afraid the truth would come out.

"Guards, arrest this man! He helped the eagle kidnap the princess!" Ly Thong cried.

Thach Sanh was heartbroken by Ly Thong's accusation and had no energy to resist the guards. As he sat in his jail cell, he started to play a sad tune on his flute.

Upon hearing the sweet, mournful notes, the princess began to weep. "Bring me the musician!" she pleaded. "I must see him!"

The king was elated to hear her speak and ordered that Thach Sanh be brought to him.

"This is the man who truly saved me! Ly Thong is a fake!" the princess cried, and she told her father the whole story.

"Thach Sanh, thank you for your bravery! You are truly a noble man and I would be honored if you will marry my daughter!" the king said. "Ly Thong you are a scoundrel! I banish you from the kingdom!"

Thach Sanh and the princess were married that day, and lived a long and happy life together.

Da Trang and the Magic Pearl

Long ago, there was a hunter named Da Trang who lived near the edge of the forest. One day, when he returned from hunting, he was terrified to see two bright green serpents moving quickly through the grass to the shrine! But when he saw them raise their heads to listen to the soothing chants coming from a nearby temple, he thought, "They are surely harmless. Maybe they are even sacred serpents."

When passing the shrine one morning, he heard loud rustling and rolling in the grass. Then he saw a big cobra, jaws open, attacking the serpents. He raised his bow and shot the cobra to save the serpents.

When the arrow struck him the cobra hissed horribly and slithered away as the male serpent chased it down the hill. The female serpent was badly wounded and soon died. Da Trang buried her respectfully under the shrine.

That night, Da Trang couldn't sleep, thinking of the poor serpent. Suddenly he heard a loud hiss on the roof of his house. He looked up to see the male serpent coiling around a wooden beam. "I am the Serpent-Genie," he whispered. "I come in gratitude to you for saving my life and burying my wife." From his mouth he dropped a shiny pearl on Da Trang's bed. "Hold this pearl in your mouth to listen to our animal language," Serpent-Genie hissed as he slithered away.

The next morning, Da Trang left home early with the magic pearl in his mouth. As soon as he entered the forest, he was amazed to hear the language of the animals, from the porcupine father talking to his babies to the yellow birds singing and praising the first rays of the sun.

A black crow flew overhead. "I see a deer two hundreds paces to your right," the crow cawed. Quickly the hunter used this information and got his first prey easily.

"Where is my reward? Where is my reward?" the crow cawed loudly.

"What do you want?" replied the hunter.

"Just your leftovers, only your leftovers," the crow answered as he flew away.

Every day Da Trang and the black crow went hunting together. The crow was always content with the leftovers. But one day there were none to be found! The crow was upset and looked for the hunter. "You're such a liar!" he cawed. "There were no leftovers for me for these past few days. Liar! Liar!"

Da Trang swore to the crow that the leftovers were carefully left in the same place as usual. But the crow gave the hunter no peace. At last Da Trang could stand the crow's accusations no longer. He shot an arrow into the air with the intent to scare away this angry creature. Suddenly the crow swooped low, picked up the arrow, and flew off, warning Da Trang as he did so that he would have revenge.

A couple of days later, Da Trang was arrested and imprisoned. An arrow with his name had been found at the scene of a crime. Nobody believed he was innocent. The poor prisoner spent most of his time begging the mosquitoes not to bite him and the rats not to steal his food.

One day, as he sat miserably in his cell, he heard voices from the ground. "Move! We need to move our food to a higher place. The flood will be coming in three days!" an ant was calling to his troupe. Da Trang saw a colony of ants crawling on the walls, carrying food. Da Trang immediately warned the guard about the upcoming flood and urged him to warn the king. The guard didn't believe the prisoner's warning, but he reported it to the king anyway.

True to the prisoner's prediction, the flood damaged many parts of the kingdom, but the animals and their food were safe. Another time, the prisoner heard the rats stealing food from invaders waiting by the kingdom's border. He shared the news with the guard, who immediately passed it along to the king. Later, the invaders were defeated.

Da Trang shared the animals' warnings with the king so often that the king ordered his release and made him his most respected advisor. Da Trang continued to protect the kingdom from floods, disasters, and invasions. The king was always eager to hear Da Trang talk to the animals and to share in their conversations.

One day, at the king's request, they headed out to the sea for more discoveries.

Not far from the shore, Da Trang heard a family of crabs urging each other to swim away as fast as they could to escape the powerful jaws of a baby shark. Then a school of sardines warned each other of an approaching sea turtle. Da Trang shared all these animal conversations with the king.

As their boat moved a little farther, Da Trang was amused to see the starfishes dancing and singing silly tunes under the bright sun. It made him laugh so hard that the magic pearl slipped out of his mouth and fell to the bottom of the sea. In panic, he jumped off the boat and desperately searched the water for the magic pearl.

For days, weeks, and months, the king sent his soldiers to help Da Trang wade in the water and shift the sand. Unfortunately, the pearl was never found. The king gave up and ordered his people to stop searching and return home to the kingdom, but the exhausted Da Trang continued to search for the magic pearl on his own.

From that day on, Da Trang was never seen again, but the villagers saw thousands and thousands of tiny crabs on the beach, scurrying and burrowing in the sand in hopes of finding the magic pearl. Sadly, their efforts were ever in vain as incoming waves would come and wash their work away. As the saying goes,

Da Trang xe cat bien Dong
Nhoc long ma chang nen cong can gi.

Da Trang pushed cartloads of sand
to fill up the Eastern sea
But all his efforts were ever in vain.

Why the Sea Is Salty

Thousands of years ago, it was believed that sea water had been tasteless until one fateful day. It started like this:

"I want to see rainbows and no more rain!" the fisherman muttered as he boiled water for his tea. It had been raining for days, so he couldn't go fishing. He was worried because he had hardly any food left—just a little salty fish and some rice.

Finally the sun came out, the sky was clear, and the happy fisherman hurried back to the sea in hopes of catching a lot of fish. The waveless sea was so calm and clear. "For sure, I will have a good catch today," thought the fisherman as he cast his net wide into the vast sea. After a while, he pulled in his heavy net, expecting it to be full of fish, shrimp, and crabs as usual. To his surprise, his net caught only seaweed and broken shells.

The fisherman was very disappointed. All day long, he cast his net on the right side, then the left, then in front of the boat. He waited patiently as he watched the seagulls flying in the sky and disappearing on the far horizon.

It grew dark, and the fisherman decided to throw his net for the last time before heading back home. Soon he felt a strong tug. "Well, the net is heavy, I can feel it." But, sadly, he found nothing, except a tiny golden fish shimmering under the moonlight in the dark green seaweed. The poor fisherman was breathless with disappointment.

"I am the Princess of the Sea. Please let me go!" begged the little fish.

"Wow! You can speak?" the fisherman cried in amazement.

"Yes," the fish replied a little impatiently. "I just told you, I am the Princess of the Sea! I'll grant you a wish if you set me free."

"A wish! You will grant me a wish if I release you into the sea?"

"Anything you wish!" the little fish replied.

The humble fisherman asked only for some salt.

The golden fish swam away and soon emerged from the bottom of the sea with a salt grinder, which she gave to the good man.

"As promised, here is a salt grinder in exchange for my freedom," whispered the fish, "Remember these magic words when you need salt."

Slowly the Princess of the Sea taught him the magic words. He thanked her for the gift and rowed back home as the golden fish happily disappeared into the dark sea.

That night, before going to bed, the fisherman took out the salt grinder and started to utter the magic words, "Salt grinder, magic salt grinder, make me some salt—just enough for the day!" He repeated it three times. Then, as he uttered the last word of the spell, clean white salt poured out from the salt grinder. When he had enough salt, the fisherman commanded, "Salt grinder, magic salt grinder. I have enough for the day. Please stop making salt." He repeated it again three times.

Since that day, the fisherman made salt to sell at the market in exchange for his daily meals. He was also kind, and made enough salt to share with needy families. It wasn't too long before a greedy man heard about the fisherman who became so well-off overnight. He eagerly wanted to know where the salt coming from, and he wanted to harvest the salt himself.

One evening, the greedy man secretly followed the fisherman home. He waited in the dark, peeping through the window. Suddenly he heard the fisherman's footsteps going towards the kitchen. He quickly stole up to the thatched kitchen wall and stood with his ear against it. He heard the fisherman say "Salt grinder, magic salt grinder, make me some salt enough for the day!" The fisherman repeated the spell three times.

To the greedy man's amazement, mounds of white salt kept pouring out from the salt grinder. "If I had this salt grinder, I would be the richest merchant in all the villages," the man thought to himself. The wicked man waited and waited

until the fisherman fell asleep. He crept back to the house as soon as he heard the fisherman snoring.

It was too dark for the man to see anything. "Where does he keep the salt grinder? It could be anywhere!" the man muttered anxiously. At last he found the magic salt grinder in the kitchen cabinet. He snatched it and ran away as fast as he could. Finally, he reached his boat and hurriedly rowed away.

When he reached in the middle of the sea, the merchant stopped rowing, wanting to see the magic. He took out the salt grinder and started to utter the magic words, "Salt grinder, magic salt grinder, make me some salt enough for

the day!" He remembered to repeat it three times. Under the moonlight, the clear, white grains poured out from the salt grinder. Pleased, the greedy man, closed his eyes and thought of buying more farm houses, a bigger boat and, of course, a nice mansion. He vowed to be the richest man in all the villages.

As he went on dreaming, the salt filled his boat, which rocked with its great weight. Water rushed in and the boat was flooded. The man awoke, but it was too late. The salt grinder kept pouring out more and more salt. "Stop! Stop!" the greedy man screamed frantically. "Stop making salt!" Alas, these were not the magic words that would stop the salt grinder. "Help me, help me!" cried the greedy man as his wooden boat began to sink, carrying him and the salt grinder to the bottom of the sea.

And so, to this day, the sea is salty—for the magic salt grinder never stops grinding salt from the depths of the ocean.

The Legend of the Mosquito

Long ago in a small thatched cottage Ngoc Tam, a gentle and modest farmer, lived with his beautiful wife Nhan Diep. Ngoc Tam loved his wife dearly and worked hard in the mulberry fields to make her happy. But Nhan Diep was never happy or satisfied.

"I don't deserve this poor and boring life," Nhan Diep muttered as she fed fresh mulberry leaves to the silkworms. The selfish wife thought more and more about fine clothes, fine jewels and a grand house. As time went on, she thought of nothing else.

One hot summer, the young wife grew very ill and passed away. Poor Ngoc Tam wept day and night. He didn't want to bury his wife, for he thought that there must be some way to bring her back to life. Soon the smell of death spread throughout the neighborhood. To spare his neighbors Ngoc Tam sold his cottage and possessions. He bought a sampan and sailed away with his wife's coffin.

He rowed for days and days along the long river without knowing where he was going. He grew very tired from rowing and weeping, and was unable to eat or drink. Finally, weak and exhausted, Ngoc Tam fell asleep. As he dozed soft voices in his head said "Ngoc Tam, why do you want to save this vain woman? Let her go, let her go..."

Bump! Suddenly the sampan hit a big rock and woke the poor man with a jolt. The farmer was amazed to find himself at the bottom of a big hill. "How long was I sleeping, and where is this place?" he asked himself. He had never seen such a green and beautiful mountain. He found himself walking among tall trees and inhaling the sweet fragrance of flowers and fruits. He brushed past dark green ferns and could hear the splashing and rushing sounds of waterfalls.

Ngoc Tam contemplated his beautiful surroundings as he went further and further uphill. Just as he thought of turning back he was startled by the sudden appearance of a tall old man. His hair and long beard were as white as snow. His eyes were bright and cheerful, and he carried a handful of fresh and fragrant herbs. Ngoc Tam realized that that he was on the mountain known as Thien Thai, and that the old man was the Genie of Medicine, who traveled the world to cure sick people.

Ngoc Tam fell on his knees and begged the genie to bring his wife back to life, promising to do anything for him in exchange. The genie replied, "I am touched and moved by your loyalty and good heart, so I stopped my mountain on your route in the hope that you would become my pupil and help me to save lives."

The poor farmer thanked the genie for his kindness and generosity, but he said, "I dedicate my whole life to loving, protecting, and caring for my wife. The moment she took her last breath, I vowed that I would be with her forever. I am destined to be her loving husband." The genie was truly sorry that this good man was wasting his devotion on such a thankless woman. "I am afraid that she won't deserve your love and trust," said the genie. "I will bring your wife back to life, but I hope you won't regret it later."

Happy and excited by the genie's words, Ngoc Tam ran down the hill and carried his wife's coffin back up the mountain. The genie ordered Ngoc Tam to open the coffin, prick the tip of his finger and let three drops of blood fall on his wife's cold body.

As soon as the third drop of blood touched Nhan Diep, the woman stirred, blinked, opened her eyes fully and smiled broadly at her husband. Ngoc Tam thanked the genie for granting his wish. The genie looked at Nhan Diep and said, "With your husband's true love and devotion, remember to place loyalty and faithfulness first. I wish you both a happy marriage."

On the way back to the village, Nhan Diep became angry when she realized that her new home was nothing but a tiny boat. The loving husband kept rowing and rowing until he felt his stomach rumble. He decided to stop by the market nearby and buy some food.

"Stay here and rest. I'll buy some crabs, fresh fish, and vegetables for a big feast to celebrate our reunion," Ngoc Tam said happily to his wife.

"Don't forget to buy new clothes, a new comb, and a red scarf for me," Nhan Diep quickly replied.

The harbor was busy with boats and ships pushing out and coming back. Soon, a large ship heading towards the shore anchored next to the little sampan.

A rich merchant in silk clothing stepped out of his cabin. He was pleased with Nhan Diep's beauty and invited her to his ship for some tea.

The faithless, greedy wife was overjoyed to meet such a rich man. She let the merchant take her away on his boat.

As the hour grew late, Ngoc Tam rushed back to the harbor to find that his beautiful wife was gone! Every day, the poor farmer rowed along the river to look for her. One day, he spotted her stepping out from a cabin of the big ship. She was richly dressed and more beautiful than ever. He called out to her and smiled at her. But she was not glad to see him. "Go away, leave me alone!" She shouted. "I will stay with the rich merchant! I won't go back to raise silkworms and live a poor life!" The poor farmer now knew that his wife would always be ungrateful and unfaithful despite his true love. His heart was broken, and his mind recalled the genie's words. He deeply regretted not heeding the genie's advice.

"If you don't love me anymore, give me back my three drops of blood and you can be free," Ngoc Tam said. Nhan Diep couldn't believe how easy it would be to make this innocent man leave her to her chosen life. She eagerly grabbed a knife and pricked her finger. As soon as the third drop of blood reached the deck, the vain woman's face turned pale, and she collapsed on the floor and died.

But the greedy woman didn't want to leave the world, so she came back to earth as a mosquito. She searched for Ngoc Tam day and night, trying to take back his three drops of blood so she could live again. But Ngoc Tam was nowhere to be found. Ever since, mosquitos have been the most annoying pests on earth, especially in Vietnam.

Why Ducks Sleep on One Leg

Have you ever wondered why ducks stand on one leg and tuck the other up under their feathers when resting or sleeping? They also have the habit of sleeping with their heads turned around backwards, nestled into their feathers, keeping one eye open to watch for predators.

According to legend, there were three ducks who were born with only one leg. They couldn't run as fast as hens and roosters, and they had a hard time finding food. They also couldn't chase after the beavers, who had two large webbed feet to help them swim fast and a large tail to help them steer.

The poor ducks limped all over the rice fields until, one day, they tried to figure out why the Jade Emperor had given them only one leg, instead of two or four, like the other animals on earth. They were not pleased.

"What's the matter with the Emperor? Did he make us this way on purpose, or did he just forget to give us the other leg?" asked the youngest duck.

The second duck stood up high, looked around, and said, "Yes, we're the only one-legged creatures on earth. We should have been created equal with the others. No one should be like us, stuck with only one leg. We struggle every single day."

The oldest and wisest duck agreed. "By all means, we should meet the Jade Emperor and ask for fairness and equality. He should give us another leg."

While the three one-legged ducks discussed their plans to see the Jade Emperor, the rooster passed by and tried to listen to every single word. The ducks wanted to know where to find the Jade Emperor so that they could bring a grievance.

"First, we need to fly up there," the little duck pointed his wing up in the air, "And I don't think any of us can fly that high."

"Oh no, I remember now," said the second duck, "Each year, the carps swim upstream and leap over the golden gate to be transformed into a dragon who protects the Jade Emperor in the celestial palace."

"But, brother," the little duck said worriedly, "how can we swim upstream like the carps?"

"Calm down, buddies!" said the oldest duck, "I suggest that we draft a letter first."

"Oh, no! None of us have experience writing a letter. We would have to consult someone!" the second duck argued.

As the three hopeless friends struggled to solve their problem, Mr. Rooster came out from the haystack and said, "Don't worry, I'll help you draft a petition. And you don't need to fly up into the sky or swim upstream to meet the Jade Emperor."

The ducks couldn't believe their luck. Mr. Rooster would be a great consultant! Within minutes, the rooster finished scribbling a letter of grievance. He passed it to the oldest duck and suggested that they meet the guardian of the village temple, who would help them convey the letter to the Jade Emperor. "Hurry up and go to the village temple. It's about a three-hour walk from here, so better scoot!" Mr. Rooster urged.

"Thank you, thank you from the bottom of our hearts! We will never forget your kindness and your help!" the ducks quacked happily in unison. Adding to their excitement, the rooster offered to go with them. The ducks were impressed by the rooster's knowledge, wisdom, and generosity.

The four friends went up the hill, down to the river, and across the rice paddies for hours and hours, and finally reached the village temple. They all looked around and searched for the temple guardian. The oldest duck held the letter tight under his wings.

It was so quiet and peaceful. Suddenly they all heard loud voices coming from the temple. "Who replaced the incense burner on the altar? Whoever heard of an incense burner with six golden legs! That's three legs too many!" The temple guardian shouted angrily to his servant. "I don't want to see these extra three legs! Please remove this burner right away!"

"Three extra legs!" the little duck shouted happily, with no notion of what an incense burner was. "Hurry up—go ask the guardian for these three extra legs!"

With the rooster's help, the oldest duck presented the letter to the guardian, who laughed. "I can understand why you want another leg! No one should have only one. But these extra legs aren't duck legs. Are you sure you want them?" he asked. "Yes please! We will learn how to use them, even if they're not duck legs!" the ducks replied.

"Fine. Each of you can have one leg. But remember that these golden legs are precious," the guardian said.

With joy and excitement, the ducks thanked the guardian and quickly attached the golden legs to their bodies.

Since that day, the ducks were overjoyed to have two legs, like other animals. They could run as fast as the hens and the roosters and they could swim along with the beavers. To be safe, they stuck their golden leg into their feathers, so no one could steal it, and stood on one leg when resting or sleeping, and always kept an eye open, because you never know who might want to steal a golden incense burner leg!

Mr. Cuoi Under the Banyan Tree

Once upon a time, a woodcutter named Cuoi lived alone in a small hut at the edge of the woods. He was so poor that in his house one would find only dented pots and pans hanging on the thatched wall, some old clothes stacked nicely in a wicker basket, and an earthen clay jar full of fresh rainwater. His garden was full of green herbs and fragrant wild flowers.

Every day he cut wood and gathered twigs that had fallen from the trees, and in the evenings he made beautiful twig baskets. He sold his baskets, herbs, and flowers at the village market.

One day, after hours of chopping wood, he felt exhausted and sat on a rock under a tall shady tree to rest. He watched the baby animals run wild and free along the stream. Closing his eyes, he listened to the soft sound of the water in the stream, where wild ducks and their ducklings waded happily.

The wind blew gently and Cuoi fell asleep. He was wakened suddenly by the ducks' loud quacking. Looking around, Cuoi was amazed to see a beautiful tiger cub chasing a chameleon.

"This poor cub may be lost," Cuoi thought. "I should take him home." Cuoi picked up the cub, petting and stoking him. Feeling warm and safe in Cuoi's hands, the baby tiger waved his tail, but still he turned his head this way and that, looking for his mom. Suddenly, Cuoi heard the loud roar of the mother tiger coming toward him. Terrified, he dropped the cub and ran for the tree. He climbed as quickly as he could until he reached the top. Down below, the cub had been hurt from his hard fall on the rock and lay unconscious.

Through the bushes the mother tiger came, looking for her lost cub. When she saw her wounded baby, she bounded over to him, roaring even more loudly than before.

Up in the tree, Cuoi watched in fear as the mother tiger ran to the water and picked some shiny green leaves from the banyan tree growing along the stream. She chewed the leaves and put the green paste on the cub's head. Instantly, the cub woke up, strong and happy as if nothing had happened. Then mother and baby scurried off into the forest.

Cuoi realized that the tree had magical healing powers. "These leaves will cure many people," he said to himself.

When he was sure the mother tiger was far away, Cuoi climbed down and picked a handful of banyan leaves and put them in his pocket. He whistled happily as he walked home.

On the way, he spotted a dog lying dead in the middle of the road. Cuoi made a paste from the leaves in his pocket, as he had seen the mother tiger do, and put the paste on the dog's head. Miraculously, the dog woke up, wagged his tail, and started barking.

85

"Tonight you'll come home with me and tomorrow we'll go back to the forest to bring the magical tree home," said Cuoi to his new companion.

The next day, the woodcutter and his dog returned to the forest with a shovel. Cuoi spent hours and hours uprooting the tree. As he carried it home, he whispered to his dog, "It is truly a magical tree. I will plant it in a pure place in my garden, near the wishing well."

The banyan tree grew and grew. Every morning Cuoi tended his garden, watered the magic tree with clean water, and never forgot to pick a great handful of leaves to carry with him wherever he went. One day, as he passed by a nearby village, he heard terrible crying and commotion from a beautiful house belonging to a wealthy merchant. Cuoi learned that the merchant's daughter was very ill and had been unable to eat, hear, or speak for many days. None of the great medicine men in the village could help her. Her family and friends were in despair.

Cuoi made a paste from the leaves in his pocket and put the paste on the girl's forehead. Within seconds the girl blinked her eyes and her cheeks grew rosy. She was completely well again. Overjoyed and grateful, the merchant gave his daughter's hand in marriage to Cuoi the woodcutter. He invited everyone from both villages to a wonderful wedding.

Cuoi brought his wife back to his home and showed her his beautiful garden with its magic banyan tree. "Will you please remember to water the plants, and especially this tree, only with clean water from the wishing well?" Cuoi asked his wife. Cuoi's wife was wonderful and hard working. She took great care of the house and the garden and loved to help Cuoi make strong twig baskets.

One summer day, after hours of cleaning the hut, feeding the chickens, and scraping pots and pans, she was very tired. It was very warm in the hut, so Cuoi's wife went outside, carrying a bucket of dirty dishwater. She sat under the shady banyan tree and fell fast asleep in the soft breeze. Soon Cuoi made his way home. The dog ran to the road, barking loudly in greeting. Startled, the young wife sprang up, and the bucket of water spilled over the tree's roots. The earth started trembling. The ground began to shake and crack. Terrified, the young wife realized that she had just watered the magic banyan tree with dirty water. She cried frantically, "Help! Help! Please help!"

Cuoi heard his wife's cries. Pebbles and dust swirled through the air. Cuoi saw that the top of the banyan tree was shaking very hard and the strong winds had broken some of its branches. "Oh no, oh no!" Cuoi cried to himself. He ran to his garden as quickly as he could, but it was too late. The magic tree was starting to uproot and fly away. Cuoi grabbed onto the roots in hopes of holding the tree down, but it kept flying higher and higher into the deep blue sky, carrying him to the moon, where he has lived ever since.

Every year, on the fifteenth day of the eighth month in the lunar calendar, children in Vietnam celebrate the joyful, colorful festival called Tet Trung Thu or Mid-Autumn festival. Carrying lanterns, they parade all over the town. They enjoy eating sweet mooncakes and gazing at the moon, believing that from that moon, lonely Mr Cuoi looks down and smiles at them.

On the ivory moon under the banyan tree
There was old Mr Cuoi dreaming of coming home.

The Jade Rabbit

During the full moon, people in Vietnam gaze at the bright sky and ponder the various moon tales. Lovers long for Hang Nga, the Moon Lady, in hopes of receiving her blessings for true love and a happy marriage. Some children see Mr. Cuoi under the banyan tree, while others try to spot Tho Ngoc, the Jade Rabbit, circling around the ivory moon. People often wonder how the rabbit, among all the animals, came to adorn the moon.

Long ago, in the most magnificent and enchanted forest, there were four best friends—the monkey, the elephant, the squirrel, and the rabbit. Even though they were close friends, their personalities were very different.

Early in the morning, while other animals still slept soundly, the elephant headed up to the mountain where he could seek out the cleanest hidden springs for a cool drink. The selfish elephant kept the location a secret.

All day long, the monkey was busy climbing up the mango tree, picking the biggest and juiciest mangoes. The greedy monkey gobbled them all up and didn't share them with the others.

The mischievous, cunning squirrel spent the whole afternoon frantically digging holes where he could bury all his acorns and nuts. Dirt, branches, and twigs were scattered everywhere, and he didn't bother to clean them up.

All the animals in the forest marveled at how the rabbit could be so wise and generous. Every day, as she wandered the hills, the rabbit patiently studied various species of herbs and grasses. Her house was filled with dry herbs and tree bark that she willingly shared with others. She was compassionate, and her deep caring for others inspired and influenced her best friends.

On chilly nights, all of the animals would gather around the fire under the moonlight and share good stories and warm friendship. The rabbit was the best storyteller in the forest and had many fans. She thanked the beaver for giving the baby squirrel a lift across the narrow stream, and praised the duck for saving the ant family when torrential rains would have washed them away. Everyone stomped and cheered to congratulate the turtle couple on having their first babies.

One day, the rabbit had an idea. "We are so blessed to live in the most enchanted forest in the world. Now it's time for us to do some good deeds," she said to her friends. "Let us share some of our food with the poor and hungry who come to the forest."

The elephant vowed to find more new springs and share his knowledge with others. "Wait, wait!" The monkey jumped up and down. "Everyone in the forest loves ripe mangoes and fresh coconuts, and I can get them!" The squirrel, moved by his friends' generosity, stopped worrying about imaginary thieves stealing his acorns and nuts. He vowed to give them all away.

A genie was flying over the forest. He heard the conversation, and every single vow. "These animals with their kind hearts bring tears to the eye! It is no wonder the animals in this forest live happily and harmoniously," he thought.

The animals soon fell fast asleep. But the rabbit lay awake thinking about what she could give away, since her only foods were grass, buds, and twig tips.

Early next morning, as her friends still slept, the rabbit heard a weak voice calling out, "Please, will someone help me?" At first the rabbit thought, "I must be dreaming!" But the voice cried out again.

"Wake up, friends!" rabbit cried. "Someone in the forest is calling for help!" Promptly the friends leaped into action.

They found a strange old man near the stream at the edge of the forest. He was soaking wet and shivering. "Please... help me," he said. "I lost my way in the forest and ...I'm exhausted, very hungry, and ...cold."

"Come to our home. We'll find you food and water, but first I'll make a fire to warm you," said the rabbit.

The elephant had already gone to the far mountain to bring some water from the spring. The monkey had run quickly to the forest for some fruits, and the squirrel had jumped over the rock and scurried away. They all knew what to do.

The old man was worn out and couldn't stop shivering. The rabbit quickly gathered dry leaves, stones, and small sticks and made a fire. Instantly, the man felt warmer, his purple lips turned rosy and he stopped shaking. He stretched his arms to warm them.

"Please give me something to eat and some water—I'm starving," the man begged. The rabbit was heartbroken at having no food for the old man. She knew that he didn't eat grass and buds. Just as tears rolled down her cheeks, her best friends all returned with ripe fruits, nuts, and fresh water.

The rabbit carefully dug all the grass surrounding the fire to prevent it from spreading. The monkey poked the fire and added more twigs and branches. The fire grew bigger and bigger. The bright, warm flames shone on the rabbit's gentle, loving face. Suddenly the rabbit looked straight at the old man and begged him, "Please eat my flesh, which is the only food I can offer to you."

Just as the brave rabbit threw herself toward the fire, the genie—for he was the poor old man—caught her in his hands. "Your selflessness, sacrifice, compassion, and bravery are truly great!" he cried. "From now on, you will be called Tho Ngoc, the Jade Rabbit, because you are so precious. You deserve to live eternally on the moon palace for all to contemplate and remember."

Before rising into the clouds with Tho Ngoc, the genie blessed the elephant, the monkey, the squirrel, the birds, and all animals in the forest with longevity and happiness.

Dedication

For my father Tran Minh Y, in memoriam, and to my family: my mom, parents-in-law, siblings, nieces, nephews, husband Thinh and children Thuy Duong, Viet Duong, Hai Duong, and Nam Duong, with love.

—*Tran Thi Minh Phuoc*

Some of these stories have been a part of our lives since we were very young, having been told to us many times by our *ba noi* and *ba ngoai*. Everything changes. Everything passes with time. But our memories of our mothers and grandmas remain. We hope that the images in this book will convey their imagination, affection, and pride to our children and grandchildren.

—*Nguyen Thi Hop and Nguyen Dong*